GW01572142

Sexual Healing: Anointed but Addicted

Sexual Healing
Anointed but Addicted

Deborah Moba

Copyright © 2020Deborah Moba

Sexual Healing: Anointed but Addicted

DISCLAIMER

The information in this book is designed to provide helpful insight on sexual healing. All information discussed and shared is true and complete to the best of my knowledge. To maintain certain people's anonymity in some instances I have deemed it appropriate to change or not to mention the names of individuals.

Some parts of the book may be sensitive as well as explicit. The book discusses subjects such as sexual assault, rape, child abuse, and many more. I try as much as possible to give real-life details on my story, as well as ensure that the subject is dealt with compassionately and respectfully. With this being said I do not condone the behaviours discussed in this book.

If you or anyone you know has gone through or is going through anything that has been mentioned in the book, please seek advice and counselling from a reliable source.

Sexual Healing: Anointed but Addicted

CONTENTS

ACKNOWLEDGMENTS

Firstly, I would like to give thanks to God, my Heavenly Father for giving me this story. I spent the majority of my years, angry at him for allowing these things to happen to me, I blamed him for everything. Until one day He spoke to me and said, to preach a message you have to go through the mess.

From then I began to see God not just as God but as a Father, and it brought me comfort knowing that before anyone else knew me, he knew me, flaws and all. Even at times where I would turn my back on him and lose hope, each time he gave me a reason to keep on believing, every time I came back he would say to me *'My daughter, I will **never** give up on you'*.

I would also like to thank those around me who have encouraged me to share my story. As someone who has felt alone their entire life, it took me a while to fully open up and let people in, but in doing so I have found healing.

Lastly, Apostle Tobi and Pastor Nicola Arayomi, who are my spiritual leaders, my mentors, and my family. Thank you for your words and your prayers, because you said yes to your calling encouraged me to say yes to mine. Your teachings have truly shaped me into the woman I am today and for that, I appreciate you both. I never would have thought coming into Light London would result in me writing a whole book dedicated to my story yet, here I am.

'Do your possible best and let God do this impossible rest'

INTRODUCTION

Well, this is weird, who would have thought I would be writing a book. Somehow that's not the most shocking thing, what shocks me more is that I'm even telling my story, I never thought I would have the courage to know how to share it.

What scared me were the labels, I thought my story would come with: whore, freak, dirty, failure, disappointment. Why? Well, those were words I used to describe myself because of what I went through. You see, what happened to me invoked emotions that were raw and real, not only did they control me but they defined me.

My name is Deborah, and I experienced sexual abuse at the tender age of 4, and by the age of 10, I was already addicted to porn. This addiction lasted for over 10 years. Here's the thing some people react almost immediately to their trauma, but not me, for me it was very different. I knew what I was going through at the time wasn't right. Having to do something in secret and doing everything in your power to avoid exposure, is usually a sign you might be involved in something wrong.

I kept quiet. For the uncertainty of the outcome or result of me sharing my secret was just far too great. Somehow the secret reared it's hidden head when I was 24 and that's when I came to the full understanding that I was sexually abused.

I know some of you or even maybe all of you are thinking, why now? Why are you only saying something now after 20 years of silence? Well, firstly, time flies. Two, it's crazy to think that as I grew up I didn't register what I went through as sexual abuse, to me it was normal because that's what I was told. You had to do those things for you to be accepted. A rite of passage if you will.

It was only during the R-Kelly scandal in 2019 when everything finally coming to light. It started with a question. The very same question you're all probably asking me now, the same question I asked when all those women came forward. "Why are you only saying something now?" Then, that night I had a dream.

I remember it clear as day. I was on the train, on my way to work. As I sat on the train I was reminded of the dream I had last night where I was confronted by my past. I saw myself, only younger going through the pain and the trauma again, but this time I was aware and could feel how wrong it was. I woke up feeling dirty, horrible, and just disappointed. I tried so hard to forget about the dream I just had, I couldn't. I thought enough is enough, I called up my fiancé and I poured it all out, I emptied my heart's content. I was ready for him to call off the wedding or say he needed a break or something, but it was the complete opposite. I felt a huge weight lifted off my shoulders and that's where my complete healing started.

I titled this book 'Sexual Healing: Anointed but Addicted' because society teaches us that sexual healing, sex, or sexual energy are ways we can heal ourselves or our relationships. The second half of the title contradicts the first since you cannot be anointed and have the gift from God whilst being addicted to sin.

Growing up in a Christian household, and knowing you had an anointing was interesting, but it then became more interesting when I became addicted. The book goes on to talk about the ongoing healing process and the decisions I had made in life. I speak deeply about the addictions I had, the emotions I went through, and how I still came back to Christ.

I've learned a lot about myself. One key lesson I learned was the ability to be broken. I came to the understanding that for so long I had this wall built up to protect myself from everything, I convinced myself I only needed me in life and no one else. I didn't want to rely on anyone, not even God. Why would I? To me, he was to blame for what I went through. I constantly questioned him 'if you loved me why would let me go through this?'.

I finally broke down, I decided I didn't want to be this person who was incapable of being vulnerable, I decided I needed to be broken. Being broken is an ongoing cycle, it's the daily decision of not being in the flesh or being in the world. I decided in my heart that I wouldn't look to him as God but as Father.

*"Before I shaped you in the womb, I knew all about you. Before you saw the light of day, I had plans for you: A prophet to the nations that's what I had in mind for you" **Jeremiah 1:5 MSG.***

We look at the scripture as something ordinary. I meditate on this scripture every day as this is the scripture that saved me. Regardless of what you have been or are going through, the plan the Father has for you will never change. Whether you have gone through abuse, going through abuse, or anything at all, remember the Father loves you.

You have a story that will save lives, and bring to light whatever is in the dark. Like I said being broken is an ongoing thing because you have to break to be great!

Thank you, now let us begin!

THE STATISTICS

Sibling sexual abuse includes penetration, touching, and other behaviours with sexual connotations, that do not always require touching...

Before we get into the truth of everything. I want all of you to know that I'm not alone in this. I know I'm not the only one who has experienced this 'pain'. When we speak about abuse we only think of the most common things, the observable instances but we rarely speak about the unseen, the abuse that happens behind closed doors, the abuse the can be right under our noses. I want to dedicate this chapter to the facts, I want to bring to light what abuse is.

Abuse is a violation of another human. It has many faces and can be committed by anyone whether it's by a stranger, carer, family member, or someone who is in a position of trust. There are several types of abuse, physical, and sexual which are the most talked-about forms however, there are others such as emotional, financial, or organisational that we fail to look at.

With the typical abuser, they rarely act insecure about what they're doing. Shockingly, they don't attempt to hide or cover up the truth, they use their power over the victim to silence them, just like a bully in the playground.

Sexual abuse is a type of behaviour that is forced upon a woman, man, or child without their consent. It is an act of violence against a victim that is weaker than the abuser. People question whether the abuser has an uncontrollable sex drive but the actions committed are not only deliberate but the goal is to have control. Sexual abuse can have both short and long-term effects such as anxiety and depression, post-traumatic stress, or relational problems with family, friends, and partners. The impact of sexual abuse can sometimes last a lifetime.

It is important to note that sexual abuse in BAME (Black, Asian, and Minority Ethnic) communities are dealt with differently in comparison to other communities; because of this, it has impacted how survivors react after their assaults

The BAME community is made up of several ethnic groups and from a young age, BAME households are sexualised due to certain cultural and outdated beliefs. This leads to victims being blamed when predators target and assault them.

For example: from a young age, the way young girls (including myself) dress and present themselves are policed, questioned and the majority of the time looked down upon. I was told not to wear tight or revealing clothing when around older or young men. This kind of behaviour shows and creates a belief that the predator cannot help themselves when committing the assault. Rather than face the issue and deal with it, these communities find it much easier to teach females how to protect themselves. By normalising the idea that victims are the ones that can prevent abuse, it turns a blind eye to the fact that perpetrators are solely responsible thus, condoning and legitimatising such behaviours. Some people would rather blame their child than prevent dangerous people from being around them to protect them.

It is very rare to hear cases about black men & women being raped. Society has more or less exposed the BAME communities as the abusers without offering much explanation on why and the root it stems from.

Men and boys are taught to get their sexual experiences early, they are not taught the right way, they are just taught that when you do it 'you are a man'. Sex makes you a man? This is taught amongst friends, families, and schools from a young age. While it is right to explain to them the context of sex, BAME families leave this to people outside of their community.

Child on child sexual abuse (COCSA) in layman terms is 'child on child intercourse' that occurs without consent and involves a disparity in power. I was powerless.

Some people even say that the trauma of COCSA is equivalent to sexual assault as an adult. Mine was worse. Child-on-child sexual abuse is differentiated from normative sexual play or anatomical curiosity and exploration e.g. playing doctors. This is because child-on-child sexual abuse is an overt and deliberate action directed at sexual stimulation.

The 'Defend Innocence' blog states that COCSA happens between the ages of 12 to 14. This is prevalent within this age range because that's around the time puberty starts, the body is changing which stirs up a desire to 'explore.' As many as up to 40% of children who are sexually abused are abused by children who are more powerful in size, age, and status.

When sexual abuse is perpetrated by one sibling upon another, it is known as 'inter sibling abuse'. Sibling sexual abuse includes penetration, touching, and other behaviours with sexual connotations, that do not always require touching. To differentiate sexual abuse from sexual curiosity or playing innocent games there needs to be some sort of coercion, secrecy, and domination over one sibling. Victims of such tend to not be aware that they're being abused until they reach a certain level of maturity and have a better understanding of the role they played during the encounters.

"Child protection has focused on adult-child [sexual] relationships, yet we know that more than 40% of all juvenile-perpetrated child sexual abuse is perpetrated in sibling relationships".

Caffaro & Conn-Caffaro (1998; 2005) defines sibling sexual abuse as sexual behaviour between siblings for which the victim is not developmentally prepared. Bank and Kahn found that most sibling incest falls into two categories: nurturance-oriented incest which involves the expression of affection and secondly power-oriented incest which is characterised by force and domination.

FIRST ENCOUNTER

*From my cheek to my neck she made sure she kissed each part
without leaving a piece of flesh untouched...*

Let's start from the beginning 'when it all happened.' My story is simple, nothing complicated. I was 4 years old and I was sexually abused. I'm now 25 years old and only dealing with the trauma now. If I'm, to be honest, I didn't realise that I was sexually abused until I was about 24. I guess I spent my time thinking what I went through was 'normal'.

I was born and raised in Hackney. Milsted House was my block, right in the centre not too far from school and right next to Hackney Theatre. My school was small, even though it looks different now, I can vividly remember what each classroom looked like, the hall, the nursery, the bathroom, all of it. I was 4 years old when I had my first encounter, and let me tell you I never expected it.

Not to brag but I was that student who was good at everything, a teacher's pet. I made sure I sat with my legs crossed and back straight, I kept my hands and feet to myself, 'Miss can I help you with this, can I help you with that?' Yep, that was me. My older brother who's 4 years older than me was in the same school. During lunchtime, I would walk across the playground to watch him play football with his friends. It was our thing like it was a must that I'd check in with him and tell him how his little sister was doing.

One day we had a new girl in the class, me being the 'perfect' student, I offered to be her partner to help her get settled in. I invited her to play with us at lunch, we played hopscotch — everybody loved hopscotch.
Whilst playing with her I knew I had to take extra care because she was different. She had something about her that was unique. At the time I didn't know but, she was born with a genetic disorder caused by cell division also known as Down syndrome. This didn't impact how I saw her. I didn't feel sorry for her. Her looks or ability didn't sway me from wanting to be her friend. When you are 4 years old, you don't understand what disabilities are, you don't get to judge people, you don't get to look at them differently because they look different. It's something we lose as we age.

An unknown fact is that one of the behaviour concerns of those suffering from down syndrome is their tendency towards obsessive behaviour. The kind of behaviour of wanting the same thing over and over again, not because they think it's bad or good but because it's what they do. For example, a child may always want to sit on a particular chair in a particular way. This habitual nature began to develop and manifest in our friendship.

We both had grown close over the few months of her being at the school. The bond I had built with her had become strong. Every morning, she would come to me and give me a big hug and say "I missed you." Every break and lunchtime she would want to play the same game we played the day before. It couldn't be different, it had to be the same. I always wondered why at the time but I guess I know now. She knew me and me only, I was her best friend. I was her only friend.

One afternoon, we were playing by the big tree just opposite the classroom and I can remember this day so vividly. Everything that happened felt so normal at the time. She asked me to show her where the bathroom was, which was nothing out of the ordinary. To journey to the bathroom was straightforward: you didn't have to go through the entire school, all you had to do was walk to the other side of the playground and there was a male and female bathroom just there, one for juniors and one for infants.

She calls me into her cubical with her, she said she wanted to show me something. She had a secret that only I could know. She told me to stand by the door. I was trapped between the door and herself. She got close, so close to the point where we were sharing the same breath. It started with a kiss on the cheek. She stops. She tells me how much she likes me and appreciates me looking after her. It felt like an odd and unnatural thing to say, but I say you are welcome anyway. At this point, my heart was beating pretty fast and a large empty bathroom suddenly turned into a hot tiny box. From my §cheek to my neck she made sure she kissed each part without leaving a piece of flesh untouched. As a child, I had so many questions running through my head like why are things the way they are? And at that point the one question I asked myself was: what is happening, what am I experiencing?

She stops again. This time to take a breath, to look at me. I could tell that she saw the worry and fear in my eyes. She makes a face, the face you make when you don't know what to say. I remember her words very clearly *'it's ok, this is normal'*. Strangely enough, her words reassured me. I felt almost a sense of calmness, I can't say peace but I accepted that perhaps it was okay. Did I think it was okay? Yes, I did. She continued *'I just want to say thank you for looking after me, and now I need to look after you'* and at that point, I let her look after me, allowed her to say thank you.

The same day after school my older brother met me outside my classroom and we walked to a family friend's like we always did until mum came home from work. As we walked my brother asked me 'you didn't come and watch me play today?' and I responded 'I was with my friend, she wanted to thank me for looking after her. He simply replies 'okay' and we continued walking until we got to where we needed to be.

To me what happened wasn't sexual abuse. It was her thanking me, that was just how she wanted to say thank you. These were theories I told myself that day, I said this to myself over and over again, until it became normal, until I was able to believe it.

Every lunchtime after that it became the norm, she would call me or she would look at me and tell me I have a secret, and each time I would go with her, and she would take me to the cubical and she would pin me up against the bathroom door and she would kiss me, and say thank you. And repeat.

Every-night when my mum would come home, I had my routine, I would stand by the kitchen door and she would ask me, 'how was your day?', a normal person would say its was okay but not me, I would tell my mum everything that happened from the time I woke up till the time she walked through the front door but that soon changed. I wouldn't tell her what happened. I was no longer honest with my mum, not because I didn't want to tell her but because somewhere deep inside of me I knew it was wrong. I just knew that I couldn't tell her, so I kept quiet.

Months went by and from neck kissing, she evolved. She touched me, somewhere I thought no one else was allowed to touch, somewhere I thought no one knew of. I can't understand how I could forget such experiences, I guess I forced my self to forget what happened to a point where I continued to function as an excellent student.

Our routine continued, but it continued to evolve. Now she undressed me, lifted my skirt and ordered me to open my legs She began to abuse my genitalia. The vivid memories expose what areas of my life have been impacted by this past trauma. I was 4 years old, I didn't know what sexual abuse was but I knew what I was going through was torture. Every time I wanted to say something, I would remember her saying that it was our secret that no one else could know, it was like I had a volcano in my throat that was waiting to erupt, I kept my lips shut, I was burning from within but no one else could see. I wanted to say something though.

This lasted 3 years, but not because I said something, but because I was about to start a new adventure. My mum had decided that she didn't want to stay In Hackney anymore. The gang violence there at the time wasn't an area she wanted my older brother to continue living in. So she made it her duty to get us out of there. I and all moved siblings moved to Kent. It was a new beginning a fresh start, an escape. The new school I was about to start allowed me to pick my name. I didn't want to be called Toyin anymore, I left that in Hackney, so I picked another name 'Deborah'. I began to introduce myself as Deborah and left Toyin where she needed to be... in the past

THE TWO MEN

He had some sense of control over me. They both did, my brother and my cousin…

Kent is known as the 'Garden of England' was different from Hackney, completely different. I saw houses instead of blocks, I was able to walk to the shops without seeing the blue tape, so for me, it was like I was in another world. New school, new name, new everything... so I thought.

I was the first out of my siblings to start school. My younger brother was about to start playschool, my sister was starting nursery, and my older brother was starting year 7. It was something new for all of us and we were pretty excited, well I was anyway.

Royal Park Primary School, an old hospital converted into a school, and you could tell. The journey to school wasn't like when we lived in Hackney. My brother and I would walk for 2 minutes and we would be at the front gate. Here I had to get 2 busses and one of those busses was very much useless, one that comes at 7am and then won't come again until about 8am...yeah... useless.

My new school was huge and I mean massive so big that you had to walk across an entire field to get to the junior side of the school (bearing in mind I was still an infant). It didn't have the outdoor bathroom, but we did have a pool, I mean the school was pretty dope. A normal person would say new year new me, well I was like ' *NEW NAME, NEW ME'*. I was ready for this new so-called adventure, ready to be Deborah.

I made friends instantly, I was still a teachers' pet, still crossed my legs and kept my hands and feet to myself so everything was practically perfect.

My cousin who was just a few years older than me lived in Hackney, just a few blocks away from my old block. Him being the only child meant that he was naturally close to me and my siblings. It was normal for us to do family sleepovers, especially during the holidays. We would spend the whole of the half term with him and sometimes he would stay with us.

One weekend my mum dropped myself and my older brother at my aunt's place to spend the weekend and that's when the dynamics changed. I was sent to bed early and still this day I'm not too sure why the youngest should go to bed early and the older kids stay up, I mean it doesn't make sense, does it? We all slept in one room, 'we' meaning all the kids. My cousin had a bunk bed, the one where it was a double bed at the bottom and the single at the top; so the boys would be at the bottom and I was at the top.

I was practically asleep when my cousin walked in and woke me up. He came in, quietly, he softly asked me if I was okay. I answered him. As I proceeded to turn my back and go back to sleep I felt a tug on my leg and I asked him what was wrong if everything was okay. As he answered, he took his hand and proceeded to play with me. I instantly had a flashback to when I was in school, in the bathroom, with her and I froze. *'I've always wanted to do this with you'* he said *'and now is a perfect time'* those words have haunted me still today. I was so young, so naive, how could I have known to say no? That evening was a blur, I woke up the next day hoping it was a nightmare or something but it wasn't. The three days I was in that house were the three days where a part of Deborah was destroyed. Could it get any worse?

I tried as much as possible to avoid going there, going to see him, just because I knew what would happen and the sense of helplessness. At this point, I was still putting on a smile. Still excelling at school. Still being the best I could be, not knowing I was damaging myself. Every time I encountered him he would look at me as if I was a prize as if I was an accomplishment.

"Don't worry this is normal" he would say *"this is what we are meant to do."*

They tell you that abuse is usually done by someone outside of the family home even though this is true they never tell you that it could be with someone at your own home. Someone you share the same DNA with. At every family gathering, I would somehow end up in the same bed as him as he laid there satisfying himself. I hated myself, not him, myself. Could he see that I had gone through this before, could he maybe sense it? Did this make me an easy target?

All of this began to take its toll. I wasn't even 10 years old yet, but it was like I was done with my time on earth. I didn't want to go to heaven or hell... I just wanted to go. Growing up in a Christian household I was taught that if you were good you'd go to heaven and if you were bad you'd go to hell. Well, I was certain I was going to hell. I mean God wouldn't want me. I was damaged goods. There was nothing untouched about me, nothing worth keeping or fighting for.

It had only been a few years of living in the new house that I wanted to leave again and start a new adventure, ready to change my name all over again. I was ready to re-invent myself once more. I didn't feel safe with my extended family and I didn't feel safe at home.

It was normal for both of my parents to leave us home alone. They would say they will only be 5 minutes but 5 minutes quickly turned into 5 hours. My older brother would be downstairs playing a game, and my sister and I would be in our room doing something stupid, either cutting each other's hair or concocting something in the bathroom sink. Boredom can stir up weird ideas. My younger brother would be with my mum the majority of the time because he was too young to stay at home (as if the rest of us weren't too young either).

One of my first memories with my older brother is one that I remember each time I glance at him, I see it. One thing you should know about my brother is that he was a real G. Before we moved to Kent I would walk across the playground with CON-FI-DENCE, like yeah I'm going to see my older brother, none of you guys can mess with me because he'll fight you. Even when we moved to Kent, my brothers' secondary school and my primary school were not too far from each other, I wouldn't walk out and meet him but it was close enough.

At this point, I was maybe 9 or maybe 10 when my brother called me downstairs. My brother had an African parent mentality just like my father. The remote could be right next to him and somehow he'd still call someone to come and give it to him, or the most common questions my brother would ask is can you make me cereal or can you make me toast (I'm sure most of you can relate). Like bro...really? He called me downstairs, his eyes were glued to the TV. His eyes didn't shift even once, he didn't look at me, but I stood there patiently awaiting some unnecessary instruction. Instead of saying make me a slice and toast, he asked can you help me. He pulled out his manhood and asked me to rub it for him.

"Pardon?"

"I need you to rub it, it's okay don't be scared. I'll show you how to do it. Just put your hand here and rub it."

"Why?"

"Because I said so"

"But I don't want to"

"I don't care just do it until I tell you to stop!"

Do I cry? Do I run? What do I do? At this point I was tired of asking myself all these questions, I came to the acceptance that this was my life. Yes, this was my life, this is what I was meant to do, nothing else. I thought I could trust my brother, just four years older. As I touched 'it' I could feel my stomach turning, like I was about to throw up. What is this unknown object in my hand, and why do I have it here, why am I doing this? The same questions which I had now become way too accustomed to, replayed once more. His eyes fixated on the TV playing his game while I did what I was meant to do.

"When should I stop?"

"When I tell you to..."

At points I was going to slow, he told me to go faster, then my hand got tired so I slowed down. I had no idea what I was doing...at this point I didn't know about sex or masturbation, so I didn't know what I was waiting for. From the ages of 9 - 12, he would constantly call me downstairs when the house was empty, he would lay down, eyes fixated on the TV, ask me to bring it out, and I would do as instructed.

Each day was different, sometimes he would want me to strip for him, sometimes he would want me to dance for him... slowly. Sometimes he would want me to sit there naked and pleasure him. He was meant to protect me, he was meant to keep me safe, he was meant to be an older brother. Was that not what older brothers were supposed to do? He forced me to perform sex acts on him and then, once he'd got what he wanted, he'd send me away as if I got in trouble to cover his tracks.

"There's no point telling anyone, they won't believe you, they will put the blame back on you so there is no point."

My memory of the occurrence was hazy, and even as I recount the details, I fear that I may have gotten it wrong, that perhaps it didn't happen, that perhaps I made it up because how could that have happened to me, the happy-go-lucky kid. But it did happen. I know it happened because for years I wouldn't let anyone close to me, I wouldn't let anyone touch me, not even to say hello.

I was ready to end it all, I told my brother that I was going to tell mum. I was going to tell her everything. I was going to go downstairs and tell her what you were doing to me. He just laughed and said *"yeah right"* as if

I didn't have the guts to do so. I barged out of his room ready to go downstairs, he pulled me back with such force, of course, he didn't want me to tell my mum, he didn't want me to say anything so what do you do when you don't want someone to expose your secret? You threaten the heck out of them. You find the best way to convince them that whatever you say will not make you innocent but make you even more guilty than the culprit. He had some sense of control over me. They both did, my brother and my cousin. I don't think they both knew what they were doing to me. I don't think either one of them had any sort of idea that the other party was having his way with me.

One afternoon, I opened my window wide ready to jump, I wanted to feel real pain. I had become so numb that I didn't feel anything anymore. If I was to jump then the secret would be out, it would be public, I wouldn't have to hide anymore but I would finally be gone, just like I wanted. I opened my window, sat upon the ledge, took a deep breath and prepared myself for what I was about to do. Just when I was ready to jump, my sister came into the room...

"What are you doing Toyin?"

"I don't want to be here anymore Mary."

"You know you'll go to hell if you do that, God doesn't like suicide, he doesn't want you to die"

Those words triggered something in me at that moment, the kind of emotion that I had been keeping low for such a long time. ANGER. The words God doesn't want you to die got me so angry I exploded. God doesn't care, he doesn't exist, if he exists then why do bad things happen, they want us to believe that he's real. They are lying to us, he doesn't care. I went on and shouting. Tears began to stream down my face and they felt so hot. All my sister could do was walk away. I fell backwards into my bed and wept until I could cry no more. I poured out my heart in need of understanding. I was angry at myself for allowing it to happen. I was angry with my family, my cousin, my brother. Look what they have done to me. I didn't want to go through this any more. I was just so angry.

ADDICTION

For me pleasure was everything, I didn't know what life was without it…

I carried on life as normal, going from one relationship to another. I somehow coasted through secondary school and college knowing there was a part of me that was now becoming rotten. The part of me that started to grow into something big. Like when you have an open wound, you don't leave it open for it to get infected, you quickly patch it up, you fix it, so nothing bad can get in. Little did I know my open wound was my heart, the seed of addiction that was planted in me was now starting to grow and take root.

Some people think that addiction isn't a real thing. Others believe that you can only be addicted to a physical substance. If you look at the definition of addiction according to *Healthline,* 'addiction as a chronic dysfunction of the brain system that involves reward, motivation, and memory.' It's about the way your body craves a substance or behaviour, especially if it causes a compulsive or obsessive pursuit of "reward" and lack of concern over consequences.

If I was to name my addiction, I would say it was *pleasure.* We hear that word and we have positive connotations. You see the word and you see comfort, you see enjoyment, even saying it makes you feel a certain type of way (don't lie). For me *pleasure* was everything,

I didn't know what life was without it. I think at one point I allowed *pleasure* to take over my life, I wasn't worried about the consequences, I wasn't worried about getting caught. It was the fact that it was making me happy...... happy to a point where I forgot about all the pain.

I found *pleasure* in porn, sex, masturbation, men, women, you name it, anything sexual I was down with it. And I loved it, every moment of it, I loved it. The more I indulged, the more my desire for it increased. It began to interfere with my daily life.

We all know that pornography has been around for some time, some may even argue 'you can't be addicted to porn' or 'it's not a real diagnosis'. If you are experiencing an uncontrollable desire to consume porn then you are addicted, if you are letting it control your behaviour and how you are with people then you are addicted. Do not let society trick you into thinking it's normal.

Porn and masturbation was my thing it was my fix and especially during my teenage years. I lived five minutes (maybe less) from college, so during my free period, I could easily go home and get my fix. I spent hours on end pursuing different porn sites, and after spending hours looking for that fix, it would last only for a moment, and I would feel guilty. I would feel dirty, yet it felt good. The rush *it* gave me just before I....always lead me to me wanting more and more. My addiction lasted for 10+ years, I can't tell you when it fully stopped, all I can tell you is that it was difficult.

Remember when I said I was ready for a new adventure? Well, here came a new one. I was able to glide through college with my addiction and not get caught, but little did I know that things were about to change.

My initial excitement when it was time to go to university was based on me leaving the nest and becoming independent. It was now time for Deborah to live for herself 'I'm going to do better' 'this is a new me' we have all been there...don't lie. Age seventeen, first-year student, my own place, oh that was the life. I say that because I didn't have 'freedom' growing up...my parents or in other words my dad was very strict.

I remember the first year of university like it was yesterday, the ability to be me, to be new again, to start a new life. I said to myself I'm going to pray every day, I'm going to get anointing oil and cover myself because

I am a child of God. You're probably laughing while reading this because at one point this was you. I think about it now and all I can say is damn girl you were weak. My so-called 'Christian lifestyle' only lasted one week.

I found myself going into my laptop typing in those words, and in the back of my mind I could hear 'this is so wrong' 'why are you doing this?' and yet I ignored it. I spent hours looking for something that would get me that fix. Even in my university accommodation where the wifi was so poor (I really should have taken a hint) I still persevered to find what I needed. I thought I needed it so badly and if I didn't have it then it would be the end.

November 2013, the year I turned eighteen. I planned a serious night out for myself. I convinced all my law classmates to come out with me. My birthday was going to be LIT. I got a space at 'The Cuban' a cafe by day and a club by night. With only 3 clubs in Canterbury, 'The Cuban' was pretty decent. I said this was going to be a night to remember, and it truly wasn't. We didn't go to the club. The night was so bad, and because of this night, I was known as that girl that fell off on her birthday. All

I remember was drinking alcohol like it was water and then ending up with my head over the toilet.

After 4 weeks of pure embarrassment, it slowly started to die down, the story that everyone knew of the girl that couldn't handle her liquor became the story of the girl who always had the lit motives. That story sparked something in me that I never had, attention. Ohh I loved it. Everyone wanted to know me, everyone wanted to say hi to me, this newfound pleasure I found was so satisfying. Coming from a school where no one would say pim to me, where not even a guy would look in my direction... I LOVED IT and then...you guessed it...I met him.

The guy I gave it all away to. Oh, he was great. We were both from Hackney so we naturally bounced off each other. I loved the attention he gave me and only me. I let him into the darkest parts of me, told him all my secrets, we were known as 'that couple' I was feeling like Beyonce and Jay-Z. The pleasure of having someone's attention, knowing someone likes me was giving me a high.

I remember the night I gave it away, it wasn't like the movies, the red roses, the candles, the music. It was like a microwave meal, tasteless, quick and not satisfying. He became my new fix. I liked him, I might as well get what I need from him, right? Wrong! What I had wasn't serious, it was the same addiction rebranded. I began to go from relationship to relationship, I was practically a whore. I found the satisfaction in sleeping around.

Should I blame myself for my addiction? Regardless of who or what was to blame I still had to face the consequences. My addiction became a distraction. I went to university to study a law and business degree but yet I was focused on finding a way to fill the emptiness inside of me. I failed my first year of university. I was distraught. When I received my results that day I blamed myself, I said Debs you're not smart, this isn't meant for you, do you enjoy your degree? Failing to realise that the reason I failed was that I was sidetracked. I went into 'prayer mode' and started praying any enemy from my fathers' house that wants me to fail, be rebuked. I'm laughing as I'm writing this because I was a mess. I started blaming things on the enemy when I was my own enemy.

THE ABUSER

Before I knew it, I was on the floor, he punched me 5 times in the face, and kicked me 3 times in the stomach...

In total, I had slept with 4 men and I know what you're thinking, 'that's not a lot' but when thinking about the soul ties and connections I had with them, they were enough to run me mad. It made the addiction deeper, it made it stronger. I was in many relationships and each time I was thinking that's what I needed. I thought I needed a man to satisfy my needs, I needed a guy to make me happy. I thought having that kind of attention was normal.

The addiction was so strong that I couldn't stop, honestly, I didn't want to stop. I started convincing my self and blaming other factors. Sometimes I look back, and I think to myself ' how did I not see this in me' 'why didn't I see this a problem'. The addiction made me do some very STUPID things.

I remember the second year of university, I got my own place. It was beautiful. It was a new build flat on Sturry Road. Rent was £750 a month including bills, tax, parking, tv licence the lot. I was living life because we all know you can NEVER find such deals in London. Anyway, £750 for 12 months = £9000. My 'boyfriend' at the time lived across the road (literally). I can tell you right now I never slept in my flat, the longest I spent there wasn't even up to a month. I spent my entire second year in his house, while I was still paying for my own flat. Stupid right?

I don't even know how I met this guy. We were studying two different degrees so we never crossed paths but for some reason, we met each other. Our relationship was perfect in the beginning, or was it? Maybe I convinced myself it was. I don't even think I can even call it a relationship, not when it was one year of complete torture. The only time where I truly believed he loved me was when I was in the hospital due to kidney failure. At that point, if I could stay in the hospital for longer, I would, I saw a side to him that no one ever saw.

I altered my life, I cut off my friends, I dressed a certain way because I wanted to keep him. I had a routine that I had to follow every day, from the moment I woke up to the moment I went to bed and it always involved him. From the Law building, I would walk across campus to the Engineering block and wait for him to finish his class. If anyone knows me, you know I don't like walking long distances, especially if it's not en route to where I need to be. The University has changed, it looks a little different now but back then the Law and Engineering building was nowhere near each other.

He had my timetable so I couldn't lie and tell him I was busy. I had to always be on time if I wasn't, then he would get mad. He had serious control over me. Even when we would argue, I can remember the words he so often repeated,

"No one wants to be with you if you leave you'll be by yourself. No friends, no one,"
And he was right, where was I going to? I already lived far from all my friends, so regardless I was actually by myself. Even when I would tell him that I would tell people what was happening, he would utter the same words my brother said...

'There's no point telling anyone, they won't believe you'

He knew all the ways to keep me down, to keep me quiet, to keep me hidden. It started as verbal abuse, I was like a sponge I had absorbed all the lies and names that were given to me in the past and he just added to the list.

The day he first laid his hands on me, it was a shock. I'm not going to lie I blamed myself that night like it was my fault. I provoked him, I pushed him to do it. When you speak to females who have been in an abusive relationship, our automatic response is *'don't blame yourself, it wasn't your fault.*' It sounds crazy but unless you've been in the situation don't say anything. As easy as it may sound to not blame yourself, at that point that's all you can do, it seems like the only logical explanation.

In my case the reason why I blamed myself was that I knew his behaviour, I knew he didn't like me talking to other people, especially guys. His jealousy was so ugly that even though he couldn't physically be in my lectures he made sure he got other people to watch me.

Side note: If you feel like you are in an abusive relationship. As hard has it may be to leave, you are strong! Please speak to someone you trust and find wise counsel.

One evening we were at the club and that's where it turned physical. I was having a conversation with someone from class and he didn't like it, he hated it. Mainly because he didn't like the guy and had the irrational feeling I liked the guy. After a few minutes of him pacing back and forth, he dragged me away into the dark where no one could see us argue. We were shouting at each other, the music was so loud that we couldn't hear what we were both sayings. I became so fed up with it that I proceeded to walk away from him. He grabbed me by the arm and punched me. I froze. I could feel the hot pins and needles on the right side of my face but in my head, all I could think was, 'you laid your hands on me'.

Thinking back to the first attack, the energy inside me, the Hackney girl inside me is saying, NEVER should I have taken that, and that's what we all females do. It's so easy to say what we can and can't take in a relationship until we are faced with the reality of it. In reality, I was weak, I was scared. In reality at that point, I wasn't that strong a black woman, I was a small girl, a small lonely scared girl who had nothing. I didn't have the energy to fight back, I didn't want to fight back if I did only God knows what would have happened to me that night. I ran out of the club and back to my place and spent the entire night tearing down myself for what I had done.

The next day, he came to my flat, saying he was sorry and how it was a mistake and he didn't know what came over him. After watching my dad abuse my mum, I always said to myself that I would never be with a man that beats me. I said it and I meant it, but when it came to me fulfilling that I somehow feared being by myself more than being beaten black and blue every day. I needed to feel it. I needed to feel that pleasure of being with someone of being 'loved' even though I didn't know what love was.

I was beaten for 12 months, beaten to points where I couldn't even get up and even then I still wanted to be with him. The embarrassment of going to class with visible cuts and bruises meant I had to expose what he was doing, but I didn't want to. I wanted to protect him. *Just be good Deborah that's all you need to do.*

I thought the only way I could keep him was to give *it* to him, the only way that he would be happy is if I gave it all to him and just behaved. I had to give *it* to him. I convinced myself that me giving *it* to him made me happy because I knew that's what he wanted when he's happy I don't get beaten so that's good, it's good right? I mean I didn't want to be on my own. People would ask if everything was okay and I would lie and say everything was fine. I was so addicted to being with someone and finding comfort in him that I lost myself in it. Deborah didn't exist anymore, all that existed were the lies. The lies that surrounded me made me.... me, that was my identity.

The night I left that relationship was like the movies, literally. I was saved in fact. It was a Saturday evening and after my daily beating, I went back to my flat to clean myself up. I look back on that day and I believe it was God that saved me. Someone rang my buzzer, to my surprise it was someone I met back in the first year that I spoke to once. They didn't know where I lived, I didn't even know they were still in university. I made sure that where we stood, everyone could see what was going on.

After a brief catch up he said his goodbyes and left. My abuser came to flat, climbed through my window and sense of aggression filled the environment. He was shouting and yelling, saying people saw me with another guy, he called me all sorts of names, and in tears, I still tried to explain to him that I wasn't doing anything. I tried to reassure him that I wasn't doing anything, that he just came to say hi. I Walked to towards him so I could look him in the eye and promise him that I was innocent...that was a mistake. Before I knew it, I was on the floor, he punched me 5 times in the face, and kicked me 3 times in the stomach.

I counted it, it was the only way to tell myself that it would be over soon. The kicks became weak and the punches became slow, at that point I was ready to say good-bye, I came to the acceptance that this was the end of me. He sat on top of me as I laid there bleeding and put his hands around my neck. I begged him telling him not to do it, I promised him that I wouldn't do it again but at the point, it was too late.

All I could hear was a loud bang from the front door. The same friend that I had just said goodbye to came barging into my flat and dragged him off of me. I was taken to the hospital to ensure I was okay. As I laid on the hospital bed thinking about my life, I understood that I couldn't live this life anymore.

That was the end of our relationship. The end of us. It was bittersweet for me, it was great because I was finally out fo the relationship, I could somehow gain control of my self again. On the other hand, the bitter taste of loneliness started overwhelming my mind....who is going to protect me now?

At the end of my second year, I decided to commit to university as it was the best thing to do. I had to put myself in an environment where I had control over what I wanted to do. My previous routine now changed into a routine that I had control over.

I wanted to let go of the addiction for so long but it was hard, the addiction was practically killing me. You don't know you have an addiction until you want to stop, but as a Christian, it's even harder to stop. The enemy tells you all the great things about what you are addicted to that you don't see anything wrong with it. In my relationship with my abuser, all that was great was that I wasn't going to be alone. From a young age, the age at which I was in that bathroom, I was groomed to not be alone, tricked into thinking I needed someone or something with me whether it made me happy or not.

OHH BABY

I was then told that there would be a huge chance that I would never have a successful pregnancy in the future...

Summer 2015, woo the summer that can never be forgotten. Some of you are now thinking about what happened in summer 2015, you are now thinking back to what you were doing during that time. Well, mine wasn't your Hot Girl Summer, mine was the total opposite. They say when summer arrives, summer romances come out to play, along with skirts and sandals. *He* was more than a summer romance, *he* was potential, but they say NEVER fall in love with potential because potential NEVER have a happy ending.

His name was... I'm not going to tell you his name, but just think tall, dark and GORGEOUS! We met through a mutual friend and like all my previous relationships we hit it off straight away, it was like we just meshed well, but he was potential. He was the guy that ticked every box, except one. Somehow he was the guy of every girl's dream. He was a MAN, he knew what he wanted and he wanted me and I wanted him.

After getting to know each other, we decided to finally hang out properly, just the two of us. We had always hung out in a group setting but never really had a chance to get to know each other properly...if you know what I mean.

The drive to his place was long, living in Kent and driving to North London in summer, when the sun is scorching hot, whilst being in traffic, was not it. I finally got to his place and it wasn't just the two of us as we had planned. The rest of the crew were there, they decided on the last minute to have a send-off for one of our friends who was moving to America, and his place was the chill spot, you know, the spot that everyone goes to when it's time to hang out. I mean the idea was just for us two to hang out but maybe another time. We decided to reschedule and enjoy the goodbye party.

A few days later my friend and I jumped in the car and went to his place. It was 'fun' just a few friends hanging out maybe a little flirting but nothing special. It was getting pretty late and a group of 6 turned into a group of 4 which then turned into just 2. Just the two of us. At this point, I didn't know what time it was and I didn't care. I knew I had to be home but time wasn't on my mind.

Picture this, hot summer evening, a movie and lots of sexual tension. The tension continued to build up, as so did hormones. Soon enough we were kissing. Once we began kissing I knew we were both asking questions in our minds but dared not to say it out loud. It was just like the movies, he looked at me and I looked at him and we both leant in and all I remember was the room getting hotter. It was slow, it was something, I mean it was...something.

We dated for that entire summer. I mean seriously, we did the summer fling thing. Long walks, movies, dinner dates, it was probably the most romantic summer of my life. At one point during this 'summer fling' I hadn't been home, for 3 weeks straight I was with him and those 3 weeks were magical. It was theatrical but in a good sense. Our kisses, slow and deep and I could feel them in the bottom of my stomach. His hands, holding my waist against the wall and with my legs wrapped around his waist I could feel a tingling between my thighs.

Fast forward to the end of the summer and at this point we were practically inseparable, glued together, but as we all know it had to come to an end. He was offered the opportunity to study his master's degree in Canada, and that was an opportunity that wouldn't come again, so we prepared to say our goodbyes. We both knew what we had was different, and agreed that it could never work with him being there and me being here. Besides, he was still just potential and you don't fall in love with potential.

We officially said our goodbyes, I took a plane to Paris for a family holiday and he made his way to Canada. Months went by and warm summer nights turned to cold winter ones. I was back at university and I was about to celebrate my 21st birthday. Everyone plans to have this big, extravagant birthday parties for the 21st. It's part of those milestones they make special cards for, you know like 16, 21, 25, 30 and 50. So I too was planning something huge, until I couldn't be bothered to do it anymore.

Birthday planning can be such a hassle and I grew lazy. Yet the prospect of spending my 21st birthday with him on the other hand was going to be something worth planning. The plan was for me to go to New York and he would meet me there. Everything was set, my family had a place there so accommodation was sorted, tickets were then purchased, your girl was ready to enjoy her winter. It was everything I dreamed it would be...it was perfect.

December soon came. After my birthday we started drifting, I found out he was dating. The angry girl in me wanted to be petty. Even though we weren't together, he was there and I was here, it still hurt. I had to force myself into a routine, one where I wasn't able to think about him. I was still studying a whole degree, was I going to waste it on another guy again?

During the Christmas season, everyone I knew went home to see their family. I was staying in dull England but my friends were turning up in the sun. The itch of wanting to be with someone had flared up. The narrative that I needed *him,* that we were perfect for each other came back to life.

To sum up winter 2015, I would say it was rubbish just horrible, I felt a type of pain that was very hard to describe, the kind of pain that probably feels like a slow death...but we will get into that later.

All of a sudden I was overwhelmed with a sense of sadness. To make things worse something was off, I noticed that I was late. For someone has always been regular it was weird for me to be late. I quickly concluded that it was stress, you know being a student is stressful. It wasn't anything else, I was just stressed.

After 2 weeks I knew something was up, I just couldn't rule it as stress anymore. I was trying to think if there was a time during my fling where we weren't careful, to be completely honest our entire fling we were NEVER careful. My mind took me straight back to our last night together, and while the night was magical, I would sit there daydreaming about that night of how we made love. We didn't just have sex we made love and maybe made something else. The flashback was clear as day fear took over my entire body. Am I pregnant?

As I walked into the shop I was still convinced that I was stressed I mean it was Christmas. Everyone is stressed during that time, that's the only logical conclusion. I rushed home, ran to the bathroom and took the test. 6 weeks. It said 6 weeks. My mind went into overdrive and I crashed. I went to bed hoping it was a dream and hid the test where no one could find it. I woke up the next day thinking it was a demonic nightmare, I went downstairs to start cooking, we had family coming over, the perfect distraction. At this point, he was trying to get in contact with me, like he could sense something was up, and at the same time, I was trying to calculate what I was going to do.

I looked at my niece, I stared at her, and I think at that point she could read my mind, because she was only 6 months, and there was a huge possibility that there was going to be another baby in the family. My mind went into overdrive again. I went back to where I hid the test hoping it had changed or glitched... It hadn't. All I could hear was PR-EG-NANT constantly going off in my head; what was I going to do? Where am I going to live? How do I tell my mum? How the hell am I going to do this?

I finally built up the courage to message him *'I'm pregnant'*. It felt like a dream saying those two words, me? Pregnant? He instantly called me, I picked up the phone and I could hear fear and disappointment in his voice. 'Are you sure?' 'How far along', and the icing on the cake 'what do you want to do?'

I was 6 weeks pregnant, with someone who was filled with potential, someone I never really saw a future with, someone who was on the other side of the world. I was 6 weeks pregnant with nothing set for myself. The one thing everyone told me not to do is what I ended up doing...getting pregnant. We spoke and he wanted the baby. I didn't. A baby at 21 wasn't fitting into my plan, he wanted it but the decision was mine. After a long conversation, I decided to get an abortion. He was very clear that he wouldn't be able to fly back to London, and for some reason, I was okay with that. I didn't want him there, so I promised to keep him up to date with everything.

It was set, the appointment to terminate the pregnancy was set. In 2 weeks I was going to have an abortion. I kept feeling this HUGE conviction that it was the wrong thing to do, and I knew it was wrong but I didn't want it. I wasn't ready for a baby. I had a vision about what I wanted it to be like, me having a baby, my dream was to be married to a man that I loved, in our home, a baby that is planned, not a baby with someone who has potential.

One morning I started feeling some minor cramps, and the first thing that came to my mind was, was the test wrong? I kept having them throughout the week until I went to the bathroom and saw minor bleeding, I quickly jumped for joy and said yes I finally have my period, I was just REALLY late, but something in the back of my mind was telling me otherwise. I went onto google and searched, I found out that it was normal for you to start spotting during the beginning stages of your pregnancy; so from feeling joy, I went back to feeling confused. Days went by and the bleeding was starting and stopping, I called the place where I was planning on having the abortion and they told me to come in straight away.

I sat in the waiting for hours, I had missed a whole day of lectures and seminars and at this point he and I were no longer in communication. I walked into the room, laid on the bed, and said my story, explained that I started bleeding but I still wanted to get rid of the baby. She wanted to I take another test just to confirm I was pregnant, and the test still confirmed your girl was pregnant. She questioned why I was bleeding, and while she did confirm that spotting was normal she was worried why I was bleeding a lot, and that's when I saw the baby.

At this point the idea of having an abortion left my mind, I was instantly amazed, there was a little tiny human being growing inside me, I was excited, I was going to be a mum, and even though I had no idea what I was doing I had nine months to figure it out, I had a mum that even though she would be angry The amazement lasted only for a moment until I suddenly heard the doctor say *"you're having a miscarriage, which explains the bleeding"* she continued to explain why I was having a miscarriage. Many factors can cause a miscarriage but in my case this was because I had an Ectopic pregnancy.

An ectopic pregnancy is when the pregnancy is formed outside of the womb which is caused by damage to the fallopian tubes. In the UK, around 1 in every 90 pregnancies is ectopic. This is around 11,000 pregnancies a year. She continued to speak explain all the issues with this and the next step. I felt numb to a point I was able to drown out her voice. What do you mean the baby was growing outside of the womb? I went from wanting an abortion to wanting to having the baby in less than a second.

I was rushed into A&E that same day, still by myself going through the pain. As if going through this wasn't painful enough, I was then told that there would be a huge chance that I would never have a successful pregnancy in the future. That's when the bubble popped, the dream of having my own family slowly crumbled before my eyes. The future I always dreamt of was now just a fantasy.

I know you are all thinking "wow Deborah, you are so strong," Well at that point yes I was, I had to be, I couldn't be weak, I couldn't cry, I couldn't swear. I had to be strong. As the doctor walked out of the room, the noise that was going on all around me became quiet, it was now just me and my thoughts.

I laid there trying to come to terms with what was happening, did I do something wrong? Was God punishing me? Who do I speak to, what do I say? What's rarely spoke about is 1 in every 4 pregnancies end in a miscarriage and I was one of them but I'm supposed to deal with it right? I'm supposed to let go and carry on with life with the possibility that I may not be able to have a child on my own.

I spent hours on hours in A&E, the best advice I got was to let the miscarriage happen, there was no need to operate as I had already gone through majority of the miscarriage. Everything was happening so quickly. I never had the time to think about what was happening and what I was going through, but once I was discharged from the hospital I was left feeling very alone with so many 'what ifs' running through my head. I'm sure you are all wondering if I told him what happened... I didn't, it wasn't going to make a difference if I told him, all I could do at this point was try to process how I was feeling and move on.

That weekend, I bled very heavily, similar to a heavy period it was just ten times worse. Having an ectopic pregnancy meant that my health was in some sort for danger, which meant that I was constantly in hospital.

From start to finish, I bled for two months straight, and the entire process was incredibly physically, mentally, and emotionally draining. In my mind, I had always thought that a miscarriage would be a short yet intense process; I hadn't expected the long, drawn-out experience I had. Instead of anyone overwhelming moment of cramping, it lasted for two months instead.

I spent time trying to make sense of what and why this was happening. I blamed myself for what happened. I accepted that this happened because I didn't want the baby. I said YES God is punishing me for what I've done. I forced myself to become numb to it all. I buried my emotions until I couldn't feel them. I went back and forth with myself on getting my emotions back I had to figure out what exactly I was feeling and how I should feel. Part of me wanted to be angry, I wanted to be angry with *him*, I wanted to be angry with God, I wanted to be angry at the world. Even though I didn't have control over 'nature' I still wanted to feel like I was in control of something.

Did I have the right to grieve? Yes, I lost a baby, my baby, my child. I may have lost a chance of me having a family because of a summer fling with someone that had potential. After the miscarriage, I was instructed by the doctor to take another pregnancy test ensuring the pregnancy had passed through. If the test said pregnant that means the baby was still growing outside the womb, if not then the miscarriage was 'successful'... the miscarriage was successful. I was no longer pregnant. It was time to move on with my life.

OVERCOMING

For all those that that told me watching porn was fine,
masturbating was normal, that it was a natural stage in life.
You are all liars…

It's now 2020, I'm 25, I've just come to terms with everything I have experienced in life and all I can say is that this doesn't define who I am.

I was born in a time where the internet was the norm. I started watching porn when I was 10 and I can say the porn addiction officially came to an end when I was 21/22. The internet was life and it still is now. It was like a world of undiscovered mysteries waiting for me to find them. It was at the time when I was sexually abused by my older brother, where I was forced to sit-down with him and watch porn, that I realised that there is more out there than just MSN and Bebo. If I'm, to be honest, I was never taught about sex, all I was taught was *'don't come back home pregnant.'* I was never taught the science behind it, the emotion or the attachment. Even when it came to having my monthly cycle and complications surrounding it, I would ask my mum why I had complications and the first thing she would say or ask me was *'who are you sleeping with?'* Already you can see that this sense of shame surrounded this topic.

Watching porn was like a school lesson. When it came to sexual education at school, they separated the females from the males. They sat us in a classroom and spoke to us about your monthly cycle, the process and what to expect. I remember the last few minutes of the class they taught us how to use a condom, and that was it, that was sex education class. It was like teaching us how to use a condom to them meant that we knew everything we needed to know. Watching porn was the only way to teach me about sex, about what it feels like to be pleasured.

There was no holding back when watching it, who could stop me. I would type those 4 letters and pages and pages of uncensored sites would be at my disposal. If I'm to be honest, porn answered a lot of my questions, all the questions I had to why certain things were happening to me, porn was able to give me some sort of answer. I would watch how the men would treat the females and weirdly felt some sort of assurance that the men in my life were never *that* rough. With understanding came control. even when the abuse stopped, when watching porn I could control what I felt, I could control the sensation that I wanted to experience without being forced to.

Being so young and having to experience such trauma, honestly put me in a position where I couldn't process my emotions fully and I believe this is often the case when it comes to trauma in young children. From the ages of 10, you start to figure out what you like and what you dislike. You are finally starting to find your identity, your style; but in the BAME community especially in Afro-Caribbean households, you are asked to grow up very quickly whether you are ready or not. We have all heard that story from our parents or an aunt or uncle *'when I was your age I was doing XYZ,'* this statement alone forces you to grow and mature very quickly whether you like it or not. We are forced to not have a childhood, we are programmed to not ask questions and to not be curious.

Watching porn was my ability to survive or as I said in one of my previous chapters it was my fix, and then having sex on top of that was just the icing on the cake for me. I loved it, I loved having sex and I loved watching porn. Yes, there is a science to it, on how your body feels and the hormone it releases, but to me, it was more than that it made me feel good, my fix, my satisfaction. It's like falling down a bottomless pit, you're just falling, the deeper you go the harder it is for you to come back up.

The outcome of my previous sexual encounters in addition to my addiction affected me more spiritually than physically. When I moved to Kent to start this new life I was having the same recurring dream which now explains how deep this addiction was.

If you didn't know this, then know it now, the spirit behind sexual immorality is evil. The spirit behind porn is WRONG. Yes, there is a blessing behind it when you are MARRIED. But, when it's done the wrong way, with the wrong mindset, you are wading into dangerous territories.

Imagine this every time you go to bed, you have the same dream. There was nothing pleasant about this dream. I wasn't running through fields with flowers I wasn't on the cover of Forbes magazine. In the dream I was running for my life, waking up hoping I was not dead. For years this was what I saw. I would be running, looking for help, and I would look behind me and there would be a huge black figure, some would call it a demon. That dream lasted 5 years. For 5 years I had the same dream, every night.

Let that sink in... and when you want to lay down with that boy, or when you want to watch porn, remember what I have seen.

Porn is such a lucrative industry that is protected. These people don't just make videos and post it on the internet like your everyday YouTuber. These people are collective companies that have been developed to rob us all. They are not just making hundreds and thousands but they are making billions. They made money from my addiction, from my trauma. They didn't care about me, they don't care about you, they care about me as a consumer, they wanted to make sure that I was watching.

They taught me sex education. Yes, they did. I was taught that the way they had sex was the way you were supposed to have sex. I was taught that this was the normal thing to do; and because I was introduced to the idea of 'sex' from a very young age, I was ready to know EVERYTHING.

For all those that that told me watching porn was fine, masturbating was normal, that it was a natural stage in life. You are all liars. They tell you this but they don't tell you that once you start, your mind becomes attached to it. They don't tell you about the issues you may face, the same people may not be able to answer your questions. Like me, I was dependant on feeling that pleasure, on feeling that satisfaction on feeling like I was in control.

The things I should have desired from God, is what I was getting, a distorted version of it from another source. I was getting it from watching porn. I got it from masturbation. I got it from having continuous sex. In my addiction, when watching porn, having sex, masturbating, I was so attracted to what I was seeing and what others were experiencing that I wanted to experience it too. Over time I knew my behaviours became compulsive and impossible to manage. The addiction was destroying me physically and emotionally.

What I needed was healing. The healing began for me when I was able to acknowledge, that I was broken. I had to come to terms with everything. People say '*speak the truth and the truth will set you free*' and this is a fact. For you to start the process of healing, you need to admit that you need it. You need to admit that you are hurt or broken. In my case, I had to admit that I was addicted.

I had to realise that there was life beyond watching porn. Since I had tricked myself into thinking that no one loved me, I had to remind my self daily that God loves me. This was a deep-rooted issue that wasn't going to go away overnight, I had to undo years of images, videos that I absorbed, words that I spoke over myself or that were spoken over me. I had to change my narrative on how I viewed sex, on how I perceived love and how I defined intimacy.

The process of my healing taught me that I could never go back. It's like when you tell a child no and you punish them for it. At some point, you have explained to them why you said no, why that thing is bad for them so that they understand that they can't do that again. If you just say no, their minds will be so curious to why you said no that they will go back again.

I had to learn why porn was bad, I had to physically and spiritually understand the issues behind masturbation and sex. Overcoming wasn't something that I had to just do. It wasn't overcoming a bad habit, it was breaking down the foundation and the altar I built around it and making a firm decision that it would never be built again.

Porn taught me how to love, it taught me how to kiss, it taught me how to be something I didn't want to be; and when you've had something teach you for 10 years, it's already engraved in your mind. I had to remove myself from certain conversations, I had to stop myself from watching certain movies. At one point I even stopped talking to men. It may sound so dramatic but think about it this way. If you are trying to lose weight, are you going to go and sit down in McDonald's and order a salad? No, you are not, the temptation that's around you will be to too much for you to say no to a five-piece select meal.

I had to consciously take physical emotions out of the equation so my soul and heart could heal. I made the mental and physical decision to change. I wanted to protect myself. I was training my mind, body and soul to be strong, that I didn't need porn, sex, or men to feel needed or to feel satisfied.

I addressed my past, I addressed the people, I sat with people I looked up to, I spoke to my Pastor, I made sure I engaged in vulnerable conversations that allowed me to relate everything that has been built in my mind. I'm on a contentious journey when it comes to my healing. I'm constantly breaking my flesh down every day so I don't sink back into those desires.

I HATE YOU

I couldn't control how I was treated. I couldn't control my miscarriage. I can't even control tomorrow; but one thing I can control is how I respond to the abuse.

I hate you
I hate that girl
I hate you, my brother, you were supposed to protect me
I hate you, my abuser, not only did you beat me but
destroyed me I hate you, Deborah, yes you, you let this
happen to yourself.
How could you? I. Hate. You.

I'm not afraid to use the word hate. The definition of the word hate as seen in the dictionary is to have an intense dislike for something or someone. I hated everyone and everything, I hated the sound of laughter, I hated the feeling of love and warmth. I hated it all. I had no right to enjoy those things, I had no authority to be happy. To be honest, I didn't want to be happy, I became so comfortable with the hate inside of me that I didn't want to be happy. My famous one line that I would say to everyone *'I'm comfortable with being on my own'*. When people would question why I didn't smile or why I was so closed off and reserved I would respond with that same line, and keep it moving. There was no way you were going to get me to smile or even say *'hi'*. The negative feelings I had towards the people from my past only got stronger as the bad experiences piled up.

The reason why I hated people so much was because of fear, fear was the underlying factor for my hatred towards people and myself. The science behind fear and hate all comes from the brain. When we see something that is different or someone we don't know or go to a place we have never been, there is an area in our brain that flares up. This emotional reaction can spark a long term pattern of dislike when it's validated by action.

Growing up in a Christian household we were always taught love, in *my household* it was just taught, never experienced. Fake love where you hate everyone on the inside but the outside, you say '*Jesus loves you*' with our entire being. I remember one of my earlier visits to the Sunday service at my current church Light London, Apostle Tobi (my now spiritual father) preached a message on offence, and at that time I was still sussing him out so I automatically switched my brain off.

'Anyone can say, "I love God," yet have hatred toward another believer. This makes him a phoney, because if you don't love a brother or sister, whom you can see, how can you truly love God, whom you can't see?' **1 John 4:20.**

Excuse me? What did he just read? What did he just say? Was he speaking to me? Was he judging me? I love you God, but are you telling me that I don't love you because I don't love others. It was like I had to remind God of everything that happened. I spent that entire service arguing with him. God you know what happened to me, you saw everything, so how can I love? How can you tell me that I don't love you because I don't love others? Then I heard the next scripture.

'For he has given us this command: whoever loves God must also demonstrate love to others' **1 John 4:21**.

So you are telling me no matter what has happened, no matter how many times people hurt me, I have to love? I laughed. That could never happen, I refuse. That Sunday evening and I realised that I was dealing with offence, I mean do you blame me? All my abusers were getting on with their lives whereas, I was stuck, stuck in the past.

Offence or hate can cause you to self-sabotage what you're meant to do. Nothing ever destroys anything really unless it happens from inside. For example, when a bank has been robbed the first people the police will go to are those who work at the bank (the people inside). I was brought up to always think that it was the enemy, that it was the devil that caused this thing to happen to me. If I was to fall over *'it was the enemy'* and it was only until I understood the meaning of offence that I started looking at what I was doing as well as the enemy.

I spent many years angry with people, I had the power to be angry, some may say I had the right to be angry.

'Being offended is a choice.' Ugh, I can never forget the day Apostle Tobi said that it was like a light switch in my head. I spent months meditating on that statement, I hated that statement but it was very much true. I chose to stay angry, I chose to hold it for many years, I chose not to speak, I chose to keep quiet.

I've realised over time, that I couldn't control what happened to me. I couldn't control how I was treated. I couldn't control my miscarriage. I can't even control tomorrow, but one thing I can control is how I respond to the abuse. With this realisation, I've been able to find freedom, and it's been an everyday journey of letting something go that once held me down. Between the abuse ending and me now, there was space and in that space my humanity and opportunity to be like Christ & reflect the Father became possible.

YES, I'M OFFENDED

I had to forgive everyone who offended me and let it go, which is the glory of releasing offence.

I overcame offence by firstly saying I was offended. If you are quick to say 'no, I'm not offended' then sorry to burst your bubble, but you're probably offended. Everything inside me didn't want to admit it, but I was. Think about it, I didn't admit I was carrying this offence till I was 24 years old, that 20 years of carrying something that I could have dropped a long time ago.

One thing I have learned in my walk with God is that pretending gets you nowhere. It doesn't work. Even when it came to accepting my call and stepping into ministry, it was difficult. I had to admit that I was wounded and bruised. Even I wanted to pray for me and scream 'JESUS LOVES YOU' it was just noise, it was empty. Not only was I hurt but I was empty.

Yes, there have been times where I have flashbacks, even while writing this book, sometimes in my everyday life. Yes, I have been offended, yes people still offend me, but I have a choice to either to stay offended and let it pile up all over again or forgive them and love them. I have to die to the physical desire to be offended.

'Your old life is dead. Your new life, which is your real life—even though invisible to spectators—is with Christ in God. He is your life. When Christ (your real life, remember) shows up

again on this earth, you'll show up, too—the real you, the glorious you. Meanwhile, be content with obscurity, like Christ.' **Colossians 3:3-4**.

I have the great privilege of sitting with Christ, I have the privilege to have a relationship with him and letting his life flow through me and respond the way he would respond. I had to forgive everyone who offended me and let it go, which is the glory of releasing offence. I had to forgive all my abusers, I had to forgive the potential and I also had to forgive myself.

The word forgives in greek means to let go, to unlock a prison door so the other person can be set free, but more often, in our bitterness, we're the ones that are being held, prisoner. Bitterness or should we say resentment is like drinking poison expecting someone else to get sick. I automatically assumed that I was making their lives difficult when I was self-sabotaging my happiness.

To let go and to then realise that God has forgiven me... no... to realise that my Father in heaven has forgiven me was the most freeing thing. He never condemned me, he never turned his back but for him to still open his arms and welcome me home shows that I am therefore able to forgive that girl, I'm able to forgive my cousin, I'm able to forgive my brother, I'm able to forgive my abuser.

'Be even-tempered, content with second place, quick to forgive an offence. Forgive as quickly and completely as the Master forgave you. And regardless of what else you put on, wear love. It's your basic, all-purpose garment. Never be without it.' **Colossians 3:13-14**

One thing I have learned during my healing process is if I am going to survive, if I'm going to do life if I'm going to say yes to God and fulfil my God-given calling, I need to learn how to release offence. I'm not saying this is going to be a walk in the park nor am I saying that you should take everything that comes at you in life. What I'm saying is LOVE. Love others the way our Father in heaven loves us, be addicted to being like him.

I finally end it here, with a public declaration

I forgive you
I forgive that girl
I love you brother, I know you'll always have my back
I forgive you, my abuser, you made me stronger
I love you, Deborah, yes you. You are amazing and that
will never change.
I. Love. You

RESOURCES

If you are suffering or going through anything that has been mentioned in this book, please do not hesitate to contact the people/charities bellow for support and advice. If you do not feel comfortable with contacting someone please speak to a close family or friend that you can trust.

I encourage you to ask for help, and speak up, do not be like me and dwell in your pain, You are strong and you are loved.

Books

The Bait of Satan by *John Bevere*

If I had known - Truth about unforgiveness and Key lessons you should know by *Pamela Simwanza*

Domestic Violence

https://www.nationaldahelpline.org.uk https://mensadviceline.org.uk

https://www.nhs.uk/live-well/healthy-body/getting-help-for-domestic-violence/

Child Abuse

https://www.gov.uk/report-child-abuse https://www.nspcc.org.uk

https://www.citizensadvice.org.uk/family/children-and-young-people/child-abuse/

Dealing with a Miscarriage

https://www.nhs.uk/conditions/miscarriage/afterwards/

https://www.healthline.com/health/miscarriage

Get Involved

https://learning.nspcc.org.uk/?
_ga=2.165321911.969541861.1598201913-188733525.15982
01913

DEAR FATHER

I thank you for the love you have for your son/daughter. I thank you for bringing them this far. The same way you love them, give them the grace to love. Father, give them the strength to forgive. Teach them to see beyond the offence.

For anyone that is going through or has gone through heartbreak, abuse, trauma, or any sort of pain, Lord I release your angels of comfort, your angels of protection, and your angels of healing. I ask you for a fresh vision for what a breakthrough will look like in their life. Help them to pursue healing. Do a miracle in them, Lord! Heal their soul and make them whole. Let them live for your love.

Lord, your word speaks promises of healing and restoration, therefore restore what was lost. I believe in the healing power of faith and prayer and I ask you to begin your mighty work in the life of your son/daughter. Please reach down and surround them with supernatural peace and strength and give them the faith to believe that all things are possible for you.

Protect them from any lies and discouragement and let their miraculous healing begin.

Amen.

MESSAGE FROM THE AUTHOR

Hey Family,

Firstly thank you for taking the time out to read this book. If you know me personally you know this has been a story that has been pending for a while. I went through ups and downs and went back and forth with God on whether or not I should write this book.

I didn't write this book because I was bored, I wrote this book because this is part of my testimony. This is my gift to you, something for you to learn from and maybe pass to others. I would love to know your thoughts on the book so please get in touch with me through my website or social media.

I'm just a young girl openly showing my mess for you to see the message. As I have mentioned throughout the book, I couldn't have done this with the Father himself.

Remember he loves you, he is love.

Printed in Great Britain
by Amazon

76703453R00058